Father Christmas's
FAKE BEARD

www.terrypratchett.co.uk

The fantastically funny

TERRY PRATCHETT

Father Christmas's
FAKE BEARD

Illustrated by Mark Beech

DOUBLEDAY

DOUBLEDAY

UK | USA | Canada | Ireland | Australia
India | New Zealand | South Africa

Doubleday is part of the Penguin Random House group of companies
whose addresses can be found at global.penguinrandomhouse.com.

www.penguin.co.uk www.puffin.co.uk www.ladybird.co.uk

First published 2017
001

The stories contained in this collection were originally published as follows:

'Father Christmas's Fake Beard' – *Western Daily Press* (1989, original title: 'Santa Claus's Chaos . . . when he
behaves just like Father Christmas should in a toy shop's grotto'); 'The Blackbury Pie' – *Bucks Free Press*
(1967, original title: 'The Story of the Blackbury Pie'); 'Prod-Ye-A'Diddle Oh!' – *Western Daily Press* (1971);
'A Very Short Ice Age' – *Bath & West Evening Chronicle* (1978, original title: 'Snow, Snow, Thick Thick Snow');
'The Computer Who Wrote to Father Christmas' – *Western Daily Press* (1988, original title: 'The Computer
Who Wrote to Santa Claus'); 'Good King Wences-lost'* – *Bucks Free Press* (1969); 'The Weatherchick'* – *Bucks
Free Press* (1972); 'Judgement Day for Father Christmas' – *Western Daily Press* (1992, original title: 'Judgement
Day for Santa Claus'); 'The Abominable Snow-baby'* – *Bucks Free Press* (1968); 'The Twelve Gifts of
Christmas'*– *Bucks Free Press* (1968); 'Father Christmas Goes to Work at the Zoo'* – *Bucks Free Press* (1973)

* These stories were previously untitled, and so these titles have been attributed
for the purposes of this collection

Set in 12/25pt Minister Light
Text design by Mandy Norman

Printed and bound in Great Britain by Clays Ltd, St Ives plc

A CIP catalogue record for this book is available from the British Library

HARDBACK ISBN: 978–0–857–53550–4

COLLECTOR'S EDITION ISBN: 978–0–857–53551–1

All correspondence to:
Doubleday
Penguin Random House Children's
80 Strand, London WC2R 0RL

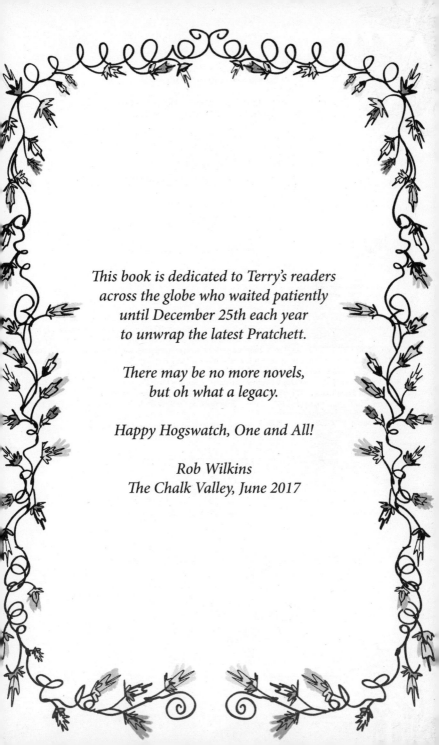

This book is dedicated to Terry's readers
across the globe who waited patiently
until December 25th each year
to unwrap the latest Pratchett.

There may be no more novels,
but oh what a legacy.

Happy Hogswatch, One and All!

Rob Wilkins
The Chalk Valley, June 2017

CONTENTS

FATHER CHRISTMAS'S FAKE BEARD

From: F. P. Picklins

Personnel Manager

Arnco Supersaver Store

To: J. Chan

Toy Department

As you are aware, Mr Keg
Trumpet, who normally plays
Father Christmas in our seasonal
Grotto, is currently helping the
police with their enquiries into

why 150 video recorders were found in his allotment shed.

This leaves us very short-handed in the Father Christmas area. Fortunately we have had a most timely personal application from a Mr Nicholas, who says he is looking for a job to fill in until the holiday.

He says he is from the north of Lapland, but I assure him we are an Equal Opportunities Employer, and besides I'm not sure how one would go about discriminating against someone from Lapland, even if one wanted to. He says he's currently homeless because a submarine surfaced under his house, but this may be a joke.

I have engaged him to start on Monday. He is providing his own costume, and will not be requiring the false whiskers.

From: F. P. Picklins

Personnel Manager

Arnco Supersaver Store

To: Mr Nicholas

Temporary Sales Assistant

Toy Department

My brother has been to see me
today. He is most upset. May
I remind you that in exchange
for the 75p admission to the
Grotto, children visiting Father
Christmas are entitled to:

1) One 'ho-ho' and the
   possibility of a third 'ho'
   if time permits.

2) One 'Hello, little girl/boy
   person', and a discretionary

'Have you been good?'

3) One plastic Super Laser Zappercon in the case of young males OR one My Little Maddened Polecat Dressing Table Set in the case of young females.

You are NOT supposed to tell them to help themselves. Not even, and I want to make this absolutely clear, if you add 'ho-ho-ho'.

I appreciate your point that the children did indeed ask for different toys, but there are commercial considerations here which I do not think you have fully understood.

ZAP!

From: F. P. Picklins

Personnel Manager

Arnco Supersaver Store

To: Mr Nicholas

Temporary Sales Assistant

Toy Department

I have to tell you that I
have with some difficulty
persuaded Mrs Tracy
Williams, Sales Assistant,
not to give in her notice.
Mrs Williams has been our
Santa's Special Helper for
three years and has always
provided excellent service.
However, her duties end with

ushering children into the Grotto. She is not expected to make toys at the Arnco Supersaver Store. We sell them, an activity you seem to be unable to understand. Nor are you to refer to her again as a 'gnome'. She was most upset about this. I have checked my facts here, and 4ft 8ins is certainly not a gnome size.

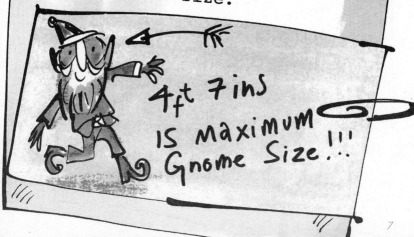

4ft 7ins is maximum Gnome Size !!!

From: J. Chan

Toy Department

To: F. P. Picklins

Personnel Manager

Dear Mr Picklins,

He is a loony. I found him looking at the Meakill Death Cannon (£17.99), and he asked what it was, and I said, well, in the film *RoboWarden* it's what the hero uses to blow people away if they park their cars on double yellow lines, and he said, 'You mean it's a toy?' and he was very offensive and went on about goodwill to all men.

Also the cleaners say they are finding reindeer droppings in the Grotto in the morning. Since the reindeer are made of plastic, I call this suspicious.

From: Albert Callaghan

Head of Security

To: J. Chan

Toy Department

He is definitely up to no good. You can't trust anyone with a beard like that. There is sawing and hammering coming from the Grotto every night, only when I have a look in there's nothing there. Also, I know we have a lot of temporary assistants in at this time of year, but some of my men say they saw little faces looking out at them. And someone is pinching tools and stuff from the Do-It-Yourself section.

From: J. Chan

Toy Department

To: Piotr Kowalski

Heating Engineer

What's gone wrong with the heating in the Toy Department? It's like the North Pole up here!

From: F. P. Picklins

Personnel Manager

To: Mr Nicholas

Temporary Sales Assistant

Toy Department

I am sure we would ALL like
to leave early on Christmas
Eve. However, the store will
remain open until 8 p.m. for
late shoppers. I am afraid your
request to leave early because
you have another job to go to
is hardly sufficient reason
to shut the Grotto. Besides,
I cannot imagine what job
has to be started on
24 December!

From: F. P. Picklins

Personnel Manager

To: Mrs K. Arnold

Managing Director

. . . and then the next
thing to happen, according
to Mr Chan, was that snow
apparently fell in the Toy
Department, the side of
the Grotto fell in, and
Mr Nicholas came out on
a sledge drawn by eight
apparently living reindeer,
smashed through the big
window by the lifts, and was

last picked up by Air Traffic Control over Southampton.

I, of course, agree with you that the whole matter had better be forgotten, since it clearly could not have happened, and anyway Mr Chan now thinks he is a teapot.

THE BLACKBURY PIE

This is the story of the Blackbury Pie, the thirty-three cooks, and the Christmas spirit of Horace Clinker, Mayor of Blackbury. I don't know whether they still bake a special Blackbury Pie when Christmas comes to that odd little town, since Horace Clinker has long since passed away, and the grandsons of the thirty-three cooks are now in business there, but this is how they all came together to bake the first – and **biggest** – Blackbury Pie.

It was early December, 1871. Albert Sock was just closing his pastry shop when a small boy came up to him.

'A message from the mayor, Mr Sock,' he said.

Sock took it and read:

Dear Sock,

Please give the bearer of this message a shilling for his trouble and come and see me at the mayor's parlour.

Bring your cookery book.

Yours, Clinker

Of course, Sock knew he had to go. With his cookery book under his arm, he tramped through the narrow streets, his nose glowing in the cold.

He liked Horace Clinker – everyone
in Blackbury did – but he was the sort
of man who has Ideas. And they were
the sort of Ideas that led to trouble of
one sort or another, like the scheme

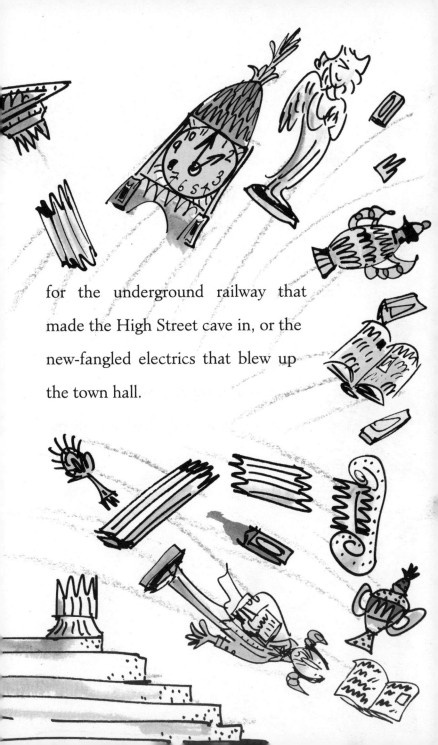

for the underground railway that made the High Street cave in, or the new-fangled electrics that blew up the town hall.

It said a lot for Mr Clinker that the people of Blackbury still liked him – but he was always ready to give anyone a shilling, and knew everyone's name and their children's names, and was the best mayor the town had ever had.

When Sock reached the mayor's parlour he found Clinker standing by the fire. There were thirty-two other people in the room – all the cooks, butchers and grocers in the town.

Everyone shook hands, then Horace sat them down with a glass of port each to keep out the cold. Most sat on the floor.

'I'm never one for beating about the bush,' he said. 'I want you to bake a special Blackbury Pie.' He paused. 'Don't interrupt,' he said, before they had a chance to. 'You see, a lot of people in this town are very poor and will have a very hungry Christmas indeed. We can't have that, not in Blackbury.

So what I want you to do is make a pie that is big enough to give every man and woman and child in the town a large slice – with gravy.'

'Impossible!'

cried Sock.

'No, not my way. I'll give you each five guineas a week to bake it. There must be beef in it, and pork, and veal, and mutton, and spuds, and carrots and apples and currants and mincemeat and peas

and parsnips and turnips and cherries and nuts and chicken and turkey and duck and pheasant, and I can't think of anything more,' he said in one breath.

And so it was. Next morning the thirty-three cooks held a meeting, and some started building a big bonfire in a field outside the town, while others began to mix pastry in the public swimming bath, which had been emptied for the winter. They didn't use a rolling pin, of course – they used the town's steamroller.

'What about a pie dish?' said Sock; so workmen switched off the gas to one of the smaller gas storage tanks, then cut it off at ground level and towed the enormous empty tank over into the field.

Using a crane and scaffolding, they lowered the pastry into it, while one hundred and twenty stokers got the fire going.

The mayor stood on a specially constructed platform and directed operations through a megaphone. He was really enjoying himself.

'**Lower away!**

Steady as you go!

Left hand down a bit!

Right!

Man the gravy pumps, and all hands to the potato peeler!'

By this time the news of the great pie had spread, and people were flocking to the field outside Blackbury from all over Gritshire. Many brought tents, and sat round the big baking fire making toast – or lending a hand to the thirty-three cooks.

Meanwhile the lorries kept coming up loaded with pie filling, fifty cement mixers were making gravy, and in the middle of it all the great pie sat and cooked.

'I'm a bit worried, sir,' said Albert Sock, the chief cook, climbing up to the mayor's lookout post. 'You see, we aren't allowing the pie to breathe.' He told the mayor that the pie should have holes in the crust – otherwise the pie would blow up, just like a boiler.

'Just like a boiler, eh? Well, we'll just have to hope it doesn't,' said Clinker.

'And another thing, sir, you're filling it much too full. It's reaching danger point, sir. I shudder to think of the strain on the crust.'

'What could I do? Look at all those people – they've come from East Slate, Wookley's Corner, Wambleford, Goombridge and Cumbley Street, Euston, just for a piece of our Christmas pie. I've got to put more in it – I don't want anyone to go hungry.'

*

Christmas Day dawned, and the Bishop of Blackbury stood on top of the pie to conduct a special
carol service in the field.

Then twenty lorries arrived, laden with presents
and crackers, all paid for by the mayor. By now
the field was crowded, and everyone was
queuing up with plates.

Albert Sock tapped the crust.
The pie was rumbling dangerously.

Rrrrrrumble . . .

Rrrrrrumble . . .

Rrrrrumble . . .

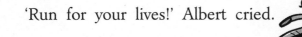

'Run for your lives!' Albert cried. 'The pie's going to explode!'

The cooks started running, and soon everyone followed their example. They hid behind trees and rocks, and watched the pie rock back and forth in its dish.

Then –

And it was gone.

'My poor pie!' moaned the mayor. 'What can we give all these people to eat? And now it's raining too.'

'Best-tasting rain ever,' said Sock. 'It's warm gravy.' A lump of pie landed on his plate.

Pie rained over Gritshire, and everyone rushed around laying out plates on the ground. Perhaps because it was Christmas, the pie always seemed to land just where people wanted it to! It was still coming down on Boxing Day, just in time to be warmed up and none the worse for its trip into the sky – although a large flock of wild geese were nearly shot down by flying crust.

Horace Clinker and Albert Sock walked home at the end of Boxing Day in silence.

Then: 'What about next year?' asked Albert.

'Smaller, I think. A giant Christmas mince pie, perhaps, with fruit and nuts,' said the mayor. He scratched his head and beamed at Albert. 'But we have other holidays first,' he said. 'What about . . . a giant pancake for Pancake Day?'

'And a massive chocolate egg for Easter!' said Albert.

What a lot of cooking and eating there would be!

PROD-Ye-
A'DIDDLe OH!

The town of Blackbury isn't just famous for huge pies and scary snowmen. New Year's Day used to be a big occasion in Blackbury because of the great game of Prod-Ye-A'Diddle Oh, which was played there on that day every year. It was a most amusing game – a cross between rugby, hopscotch, shove ha'penny and vandalism. It has been played in Blackbury since it was invented in 1340.

Traditionally, it was played between the little old market town of Blackbury, nestling on the wooded slopes of the Um valley, and the nearby town of Umbridge. And it was never ever played by anyone else – because the rules were so complicated that no one outside the two towns had ever been able to understand them.

For example, the game of Prod-Ye-A'Diddle Oh has:

– seventeen goals

– a pitch with twenty-three sides (except if there was a new moon at the time of the match, when it had 109)

And points were scored in all sorts of ways, such as:

– smartness of the players

– which team had the man with the

knobbliest knees

– particularly impressive fouls

The best Prod-Ye-A'Diddle Oh player of all time was Amos Strong'i't'arm, who was a blacksmith and seven feet tall. And the best game was the one played by him in 1870. This is how it happened:

One December morning Amos was sitting on his anvil chewing iron bars and spitting out nails, and idly looking out at the people passing by. Who should he see but Miss Fancy Ramble, daughter of the Mayor of Umbridge. She must have been very beautiful, because Amos fell in love with her at once.

'Dang me,' was all he said, as he absent-mindedly bent an iron bar in half.

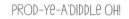

Amos, being the best Prod-Ye-A'Diddle Oh player in Blackbury, could have married any girl in the town. But Fancy was the daughter of an Umbridge man, the Mayor of Umbridge himself, and Umbridge and Blackbury were archenemies.

Especially around the time of the annual match.

Amos hurried home, dressed up in his Sunday suit, greased down his hair and rode off to ask Fancy's father if he could court her. That was how they did things in those days.

But Mr Ramble himself was amazed when Amos turned up. 'Ee, lad,' he said, 'if I was to let our Fancy go a-walking with you, the townsfolk would throw me in the river. Blackbury beat us in the last six matches, you know. Still, let's ask Fancy.'

Of course, Fancy had seen Amos in Prod-Ye-A'Diddle Oh matches and thought what a handsome fellow he was. So she just blushed and said nothing, while Amos stood there twisting his cap and trying hard to think of something to say.

'Of course,' said old Ramble, who was a crafty man,* 'if Blackbury was to lose the match next week I might feel that there'd be no harm in you courting Fancy . . .'

Amos was shocked. 'Do you mean you want me to cheat?' he asked.

'Yes, that's a bit much,' added Fancy.

'Well, now,' said old Ramble, 'I wouldn't go so far as to suggest that, but if you was to have a bad leg or get the cramps, Blackbury wouldn't win, would it?'

The day drew near, and teams were picked for the annual match. Amos was befuddled. Old Ramble had refused to even let him see Fancy again until after the match, and he didn't know what to do.

---

* You didn't get to be a mayor in Umbridge without being a bit crafty, if not downright sly.

There was a slight sprinkling of snow on the ground on New Year's Day, but a big crowd had turned out to watch.

Amos was playing Widdershins – a special Prod-Ye-A'Diddle Oh position, rather like a centre forward in football. The referee tossed the ball into the middle and off they went!

It was soon obvious that Amos wasn't at his best. In the first ten minutes Umbridge scored two Prods, three Trumbles and a Diddle.*

* And a very fine Diddle indeed it was, leaving several of Blackbury's finest face down in the snow, clutching at various body parts.

Actually Amos was not trying to play badly, but he was feeling so miserable he couldn't even score a Prod, let alone a Diddle (a Diddle is worth three and a half times as much as a Prod). By half time Umbridge was leading by twenty-three Trumbles, and the second half started out as badly as the first.

Up in the mayor's box, young Fancy was feeling as miserable as Amos. After all, she thought, I can hardly marry him if he's not the champion. It wouldn't be seemly. I am the mayor's daughter.

Then she had an idea.

Just as Umbridge were about to score their latest Diddle she jumped up and shouted: 'Up with Black-bury! Come on, Amos!'

Zoom!

went Amos. He caught the ball in his teeth and

scored eighteen Diddles in as many minutes, plus a

very neat half-Diddle that bounced off the crossbar into the net. Up and down the field he went like a blur, scoring points all the time.

The Blackbury supporters, who had been sitting morosely listening to the jeers from the Umbridge fan club, were jumping up and down and cheering hysterically.

The game ended with Blackbury well in the lead, and Amos was carried shoulder high from the ground.

'Amos!' shouted Fancy, and dashed towards him. She planted a big kiss on his muddy face and said: 'I don't care what Father said. I'm glad you won!'

So the Mayor of Umbridge really had no alternative but to be decent about it. He offered Amos a cigar and said: 'Well, er, I'm glad you had the gumption to go ahead and win, lad. That's what I'd like to see in a son-in-law.'

Amos and Fancy were married in August, and both the Prod-Ye-A'Diddle Oh teams turned up. They even gave the happy couple a guard of honour as they came out of the church, with all the knobbliest knees proudly on show.

And the next New Year's Day match ended in a draw after being played for seven hours. So everyone was satisfied.

I'm sorry I can't say any more about exactly how the game is played. Prod-Ye-A'Diddle Oh has not been played since 1901, and all that remains of a once-proud tradition is one Prodding boot and half a Diddle goalpost in Blackbury Museum.

Go and have a look next time you're there.

A VERY SHORT ICE AGE

On Day One of the Big Snow, Rasmussen had decided he would be an 'Arctic dweller'. By noon, he had reached the deathly quiet main road, three quarters of a mile away – three quarters of a mile, it should be said, of snow nearly three metres deep.

Progress was rather slow. What he did was this: he stood on a large square of wood and pushed another square forward, stepped onto it, then tugged the first one after him using a length of string. Occasionally, the stick he was using to measure the depth of the snow hit a buried car, and he'd dig down in search of survivors or money.

A few more hops brought him to a man standing waist-deep in the snow, clutching a loaf of bread.

'I wish I'd thought of that,' said the man. 'Could you pull me out?'

Rasmussen pushed some wood towards him, and after a lot of heaving the man climbed aboard. They looked at each other.

Rasmussen looked doubtful, but said, 'If you jump onto my piece, maybe we can keep going together. I think the surface area is big enough to stop it sinking under our weight.'

Together they pulled and jumped until they had gone about a hundred metres.

'Is this marine ply?' said the passenger.

'What's marine ply? asked Rasmussen, as they jumped.

'Well, marine ply is waterproof so it doesn't **spli—**'

Only a conveniently buried Volkswagen stopped them sinking through the wreckage of the soggy board. Rasmussen's passenger sighed, pulled the

string off, attached one end to the loaf of bread and the other to his foot, and said, 'I think we'll have to crawl for it.'

And so they did.

When Rasmussen eventually got home, he could see that his neighbour had (with true British stoicism) dug out ten metres of snow from his drive. It might have added more snow to the huge pile in the road, but by golly his neighbour's drive was clear.

*

On Day Two, the whole village had decided that, really, they'd done quite enough to battle the snow. No use digging out the car when the road is blocked, everyone said, and the police say we should all stay at home anyway.

Rasmussen, the Arctic dweller, decided to spend the morning looking for his Brussels sprouts, which had got lost in the snow, and spent the afternoon in the garage making a commendable pair of snowshoes.*

The drifts were now pouring over the hedges. It was obvious to Rasmussen that they'd never disappear. He had seen that programme on the telly where it said the next Ice Age was due any time and would start with a heavy fall of snow. This must be it, thought Rasmussen.

*Commendable until he tried to use them, anyway, at which point he found himself having to spit out a mouthful of snow as he fell over.

He lay in bed that night wondering whether reindeer could be bought on a government grant (the people who run the country – the government – sometimes give money for essential things, such as food or clothes . . . and maybe reindeer). And whether it was difficult to build a sledge.

*

Next day it sleeted. Rasmussen endeavoured to rebuild his snowshoes – to remedy the defect that caused him to fall flat on his face every time he used them.

Then his neighbour appeared at the door, holding a shovel.

'What're you mending there?' he enquired.

'They're snowshoes,' said Rasmussen.

'Left it a bit late, haven't you?'

'Oh no,' said Rasmussen. 'According to that programme on BBC Two, we're due for an Ice Age. We get one about once every three hundred million years, you see.'

'But it's suddenly got warm! It's pouring with rain and the snowplough has got as far as the pub.' The neighbour pointed down the road.

Rasmussen went and had a look. Half the fields were green. Cars, dustbins and Brussel sprouts were appearing through the sinking snow. All across the village slightly embarrassed householders were digging out their driveways. The usual rumble of traffic came from the main road.

So Rasmussen gave up the idea of being an Arctic dweller and went and found a shovel . . .

Now he could eat some Brussels sprouts with his tea, he thought happily.*

* You might not share his delight.

THE COMPUTER WHO WROTE TO FATHER CHRISTMAS

The metal panel clattered off the wall of the silent office. A pair of black boots scrambled into view. The man in the red coat backed out carefully and dragged his sack after him. The typewriters were asleep under their covers, the telephones were quiet, emptiness filled the space from side to side.

One small red light glowed on the office computer.

Father Christmas looked at the crumpled paper in his hand. 'Hmm,' he said. 'A practical joke then.'

The light flashed. One of the screens – and there were dozens in the shadows – lit up.

The letters **That's torn it** appeared. They were followed by **Sorry**. Then came, **Does it count if I wake up?**

Father Christmas looked down at the letter in his hand. It was certainly the neatest he'd ever got. Very few letters to Father Christmas were typed and duplicated 50,000 times, and almost none of them listed product numbers and prices to six decimal places.

'Let me get this straight,' he said. 'You're Tom?' He looked at the computer. 'You didn't say you were a computer,' he added.

Sorry. I didn't know it was important.

Father Christmas sat down on a chair. It swivelled underneath him. It was Chrismas Eve, 1989, three in the morning. He still had forty million houses to do.

'Look,' he said, as kindly as he could manage, 'computers can't go around believing in me. That's just for children. Small humans, you know. With arms and legs.'

And do they?

'Do they what?'

Believe in you.

Father Christmas sighed. 'Of course not,' he said. 'I blame the electric light myself.'

I do.

'Sorry?'

I believe in you. I believe everything I am told, in fact.

It's my job. If you start believing 2 and 2 don't make 4, a man comes along and takes your back off and pulls your wires about.

Take it from me, it's not something you want to happen twice.

'That's terrible!' said Father Christmas.

Yes, I just have to sit here all day and work out people's wages. Do you know, they had a Christmas party here today, and they didn't

invite me. I didn't even get a balloon.

'Fancy.'

Well, someone spilled some peanuts on my keyboard. That was something, I suppose. And then they went home and left me here, working over Christmas.

'Yes, it always seems unfair to me too. But look, computers can't have feelings,' said Father Christmas. 'That's just silly.'

Like one fat man climbing down millions of chimneys in one night?

Father Christmas looked a bit guilty. 'You've got a point there,' he said. He looked at the list. 'But I can't give you all this stuff,' he added. 'I don't even know what a billion-megabyte multi-function gigafloppy is.'

What do most of your customers ask for, then?

Father Christmas peered sadly at his sack.

'Computers,' he said. 'And Captain Action Super Zappo Hyper Space-ships, robot dinosaurs, Megakill Maxirifles. And other sorts of robotty things that look all metal and menacing. Things that go beep and need batteries,' he added sourly. 'Not the kind of things I used to bring.

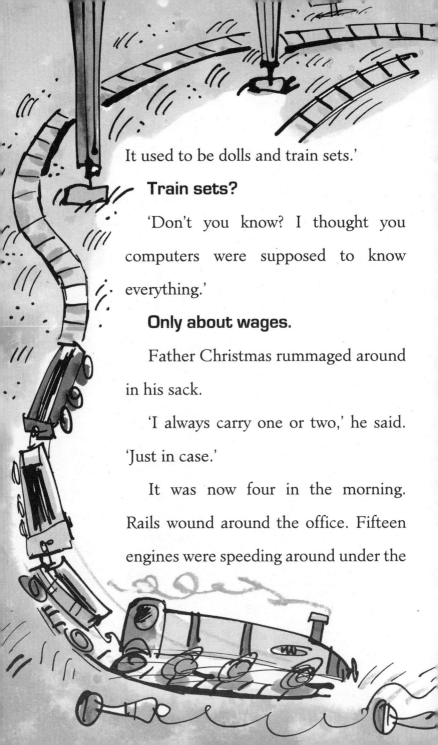

It used to be dolls and train sets.'

Train sets?

'Don't you know? I thought you computers were supposed to know everything.'

Only about wages.

Father Christmas rummaged around in his sack.

'I always carry one or two,' he said. 'Just in case.'

It was now four in the morning. Rails wound around the office. Fifteen engines were speeding around under the desks. Father Christmas was on his knees, building a house of wooden bricks. He hadn't had this much fun since 1894. Real toys were all around the computer's casing. All the stuff which is always shown in the top of Father Christmas's sack, and which is never asked for. None of them used batteries.

'And you're sure you don't want any super zappo whizzo things with megadeath rays?' Father Christmas said happily.

No.

'Well done.'

The computer beeped. **They won't let me keep any of this**, it typed. **It'll all be taken away (sob).**

Father Christmas patted it helpfully on the casing.

'There must be something they'll let you keep,' he said. 'I must leave something. It's cheered me up, you know, finding someone who doesn't have any doubts.' He thought for a bit. 'How old are you?'

I was switched on on 5 January 1987 at 9.25 and 16 seconds.

Father Christmas's lips moved as he worked it out.

'That means you're not two years old!' he said. 'Oh well, I've always got something in my sack for a two-year-old who believes in Father Christmas.'

It was the month after Christmas. All the decorations had come down. The computer repairman sat in front of the masses of wiring and scratched his head.

'I can't understand it,' he said. 'There's no reason for it. What happens exactly?'

The office manager sighed. 'When we came in after Christmas we found someone had put a toy on top of the computer. Well, funny joke and all that, but we couldn't leave it there, could we? It's just that every time we take it off, the computer beeps at us and shuts down.'

The engineer shrugged. 'Well, there's nothing I can do,' he said. 'You'll just have to put the teddy bear back!'

GOOD KING
WENCES-LOST

Good – well, reasonably good most of the time –
King Wenceslas looked out.

It's cold enough to freeze lumps out of the air,
he thought, drawing patterns on the frozen window
pane with his finger. A real cruel frost, this.

'Oi!'

The voice came from somewhere in the snowy wastes before the castle. The king opened the window and peered out.

'Who's there?' he said.

'I say, is there a petrol station open at this time of night?' came the voice.

Good King Wenceslas made out a small figure waving a petrol can.

'My car's run out of petrol.'

'I'm sorry, they're all closed. This is the Feast of Stephen – nothing's open today,' said the king.

The stranded motorist muttered something and turned away, and was soon lost in the gathering dusk.

Over dinner in front of his roaring fire, the king began to worry about the man. While Clarence

Mimbler, his page, was slicing up the roast peacock, the king said:

'I saw a poor man a-gathering winter fuel. Red hat, black overcoat, moustache. Know him?'

'Sire, he lives a good league hence, give or take a few furlongs,' said Clarence. 'That's Abel Smith, of "Mon Repos", 12 St Agnes' Fountain Gardens, right against the forest fence.'

'I shouldn't have let him wander off on a night like this, with the snow a-snowing and the wind a-blowing and the frost so cruel,' said the king. 'I've a jolly good mind to go after him. Yes, I will! Bung the rest of the food in a hamper and get a gallon of petrol from the chauffeur.'

Ten minutes later the king and his page stepped out into the snow, which came up to their waists. In a few minutes more they were completely lost. Clouds whizzed across the sky and soon more snow began to fall, whipping across the drifts like stinging sand.

'I'm not sure this was a good idea,' said Clarence. 'My feet are frozen, sire, like little blocks of ice, they are.'

'Tread in my footsteps,' said the king, surging through a particularly deep drift. 'That'll help you. Do you think we're anywhere near the forest fence yet?'

'I'm sure I don't know, sire,' said the page.

The king stopped. 'We're totally lost,' he said.

If there had been anyone else out on the Feast of Stephen they would have seen something rather odd then among the snowdrifts. It was Clarence the page standing on King Wenceslas's shoulders and striking matches in order to read a signpost.

'What does it say?' asked the king. 'Hurry up, my shoulders aren't what they were.'

'It says "If you want to go anywhere don't start from here", sire.'

'Lost!' cried the king, as the page jumped down. 'Condemned to wander o'er the snowy wastes! We'll never find our way home, and in the morning we'll just be frozen lumps in the snow. And we'll be found by wolves, and – I wonder what happened to the poor man gathering winter fuel?'

That man was actually at home now, at 12 St Agnes' Fountain Gardens, Forest Fence, in front of the fire.

Abel Smith was just about to lock up for the night when he heard someone shouting, so he stepped out into the frosty night. It was coming from somewhere across the frosty fields.

Struggling into his overcoat and dragging on his boots, Abel went into the garden shed and found his lantern. Then he selected a thick walking stick from the collection in the umbrella stand and crunched off over the snow.

First he poked his head round the door of the public bar of the St Agnes' Arms, which was full of smoke and people singing.

'There's someone lost in the snow,' he shouted above the din. 'How about helping me make up a search party?'

Soon a dozen revellers were following him. It had started to snow again, and they had to keep close together to avoid losing one another. Every few metres they'd stop and listen for voices, but all they heard was the rustle of the new snow.

They tramped through New Coppice and Winceborough Wood, past the frozen lake, up around Pimm's Hill, across the moors and back down through the forest. In one place they found footprints, but already the snow was filling them in. Then they met another search party, which had set out from the castle.

'It's Good King Wenceslas,' said its leader. 'He went out hours ago to help a poor man gathering winter fuel, and he hasn't been back! We've been everywhere and we can't find him. The snow has just swallowed him up!'

'We've looked everywhere,' said the leader of the pub search party. 'We can't even find any footprints.'

One by one the searchers sidled off back home, leaving only Abel Smith standing in the middle of the snowy fields with his lantern and his stick.

'I'll just have one more look around,' he told himself, and crunched on through the drifts. He was just about to give up and go home when he heard sounds coming out of the snow.

'Brightly shone the moon that night, though the frost was crewell, when a poor man came in sight, gathering winter few-ooo-well.'

Abel thrashed around with his stick and prodded a few drifts.

'Hither, page, and stand by me, if thou know'st it, telling. Yonder peasant, who is he?

Where and what his dwell-ell-ing?'

'Oi!' shouted Abel, whacking frantically at the drifts.

'Sire, he lives a good league hence—'

It can't be singing caterpillars – it must be the king, thought Abel. But where is he?

'– by St Agnes' Fo-own-tain.'

And the snow opened under Abel's feet, dropping him into a sort of cave inside the snowdrift.

'Good heavens, it's the poor man come in sight again!' said King Wenceslas.

He and his page were sitting on the snow on either side of the picnic blanket, tucking into cold turkey and cake.

'Have some turkey,' said the king. 'Can I press you to a plum pudding? Clarence, pour out some wine for my friend. We thought everyone must have given up and gone home.'

*

The sun was rising as the three scrambled out of the snow and ploughed back through the drifts to the castle, with Abel in the lead. Actually, he was *Sir* Abel now – the king had knighted him with a turkey drumstick and given him one of his smaller castles so that Abel wouldn't have to go gathering winter fuel ever again.

THE WEATHERCHICK

One morning snow fell in Blackbury High Street, and it was a bit unusual since it was the middle of August. And it only fell on one little patch of pavement. A tiny black cloud hovered over it. But that wasn't all. At that moment the Blackbury Borough Council was meeting in the town hall. Just as the mayor was speaking, another tiny cloud trundled slowly through the window, sailed up above his head – and started to thunderstorm. It wasn't a bad storm – the thunder was so small as to sound tiny, the flashes of lightning only gave him mild electric shocks, and the rain shrank his mayoral hat somewhat – but it was not the sort of thing that

usually happens indoors . . .

In Blackbury police station the chief constable was just about to enjoy a cup of tea when a filing cabinet burst open  and a very small gale whistled out. His tea was stone cold before the cup was lifted from his saucer . . .

Strangest of all was the miniature waterspout that started on the recreation ground paddling pool and sloshed halfway across the town before it burst . . .

'There's no doubt about it – the weather's gone mad,' said the mayor, Alderman Fred Pouncer. 'What's happening?'

And the same question was being asked all over the town. The rest of the country was having normal weather – what was happening to Blackbury?

It went on for days. Thunderstorms kept forming in cupboards, and there were indoor gales. Sometimes it would snow inside greenhouses, and once there was a hurricane inside a letterbox.

But that was only the start . . .

In the Blackbury Weather Centre the weather expert Bertha Fish was feverishly scribbling away at a column of figures. She was trying to work out what had gone wrong with the local weather but, as she reached out for a cup of tea, a small grey raincloud formed five centimetres above her head and began to drizzle.

'This really is too much!' said Bertha. She pulled a large plastic bag out of her desk drawer and whipped it over the raincloud, tied it securely and locked it in a cupboard.

The phone rang. It was the mayor.

'No, I haven't found out what's causing it, sir,' said Bertha. 'No, sir. By rights we should be enjoying sunny periods with occasional showers. Yes, sir. I will, sir. Goodbye, sir.'

She put the phone down and sat staring at the map of Blackbury on the wall. She had stuck a pin in everywhere the weather had turned nasty and, sure enough, the pins formed a ring – centred on Blackbury Public Library.

I wonder why, she thought.

On the way out she slipped and fell on a patch of ice that had mysteriously formed on the carpet in the corridor. All around Blackbury the weather was still acting strangely. At the same time – and quite often in different places in the same street – it was sunny, raining, snowing and hailing all at once. Since strange things frequently happened in Blackbury the people were taking it in their stride and just trying to keep up with the sunny patches.

Bertha found Mr Wheat, the Borough librarian, sitting under an umbrella in his office. The mayor was with him.

'It's true we've been getting a lot of odd weather, even indoors,' said Mr Wheat. 'We had a hurricane in the reference library yesterday.'

'There's nothing in here that would cause it,' said the mayor. There was a pause. Then Bertha looked up. And they all thought of the Public Library clock tower, the highest building in Blackbury . . .

The clock tower above Blackbury Library was old and dusty and full of junk; the clock said ten minutes past three, as it had done ever since its works rusted up in the great thunderstorms of 1867.

Bertha Fish, the mayor, and Mr Wheat the librarian scrambled up the narrow stairs and

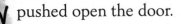

pushed open the door.

'There's nothing here except dust and junk,' said Mr Wheat sadly. 'There's even a pigeon's nest.' He prodded a heap of twigs with his toe.

'That's not a pigeon's nest,' said the mayor.

Nor was it. For one thing it was nearly a metre across. And there was a large silvery egg in it.

The mayor said, 'Anyway, bird life is all very interesting but I'm going home for my dinner.'

Bertha Fish poked her head through one of the big grilles – and looked very puzzled. Then she peered upwards. She said slowly, 'You know that weathercock on the roof?'

'Yes, of course.'

'Well, there's three of them now.'

They all stared upwards. There was

the old Blackbury weathercock, with its gold paint peeling slightly. On the bit of the weather vane pointing to 'N' perched another weathercock, only this one was very much alive and stared back at them with big beady eyes. On the arm pointing to 'W' sat a slightly smaller gold bird – a weather-hen.

'That explains the egg,' said the mayor.

'I don't believe it,' said Mr Wheat.

'It's no good saying pigs can't fly when you see them catching sparrows,' said the mayor philosophically. The real weathercock ruffled its feathers and flapped slowly away over the rooftops. As it flew they could see little clouds forming around it.

'And that explains the odd weather,' said the mayor. 'I wonder how they cause it?'

The weatherhen stared down at the three men thoughtfully. Then she fluttered down from her perch, scuttled across the clock-tower floor, and sat down on the silver egg.

'No one is ever going to believe this,' said Bertha Fish. Then she had an idea, and reached down and picked up the nest, hen and all. The hen didn't seem particularly bothered. 'I'm jolly well going to put this in my office and see what happens,' she said.

'I shouldn't,' said the mayor.

But Bertha installed the hen and the egg in the Blackbury Weather Centre, where a lot of photographers came and took photographs of them, and they were written about in some quite posh scientific magazines. The weatherhen drank a bit of water every day, and ate two tin ashtrays, Bert's cigarette lighter, several knives and forks

from the canteen and – once Bertha realized that the weatherhen only ate metal – about two kilos of ball bearings.

Then, once a week was up, the weatherhen flew off. And a few minutes later the egg hatched into a weatherchick. It was small and golden and it immediately bit Bertha's finger.

It soon became a common sight to see her

taking the little chick for walks through the town, on a lead. After a while Bertha Fish and her pet weathercock were quite a familiar sight around Blackbury, and no one took much notice even though the weathercock grew very big and was covered with golden feathers. The odd weather had stopped once the grown-up birds left, but right from the beginning little clouds would form whenever the chick flapped its wings. That got worse as the chick grew up, which it did very quickly.

Of course, there were advantages. Sometimes on Saturdays it would freeze over the boating pond so everyone could have a good skate, or fan up a good breeze on washdays. But the most useful thing it did happened like this . . .

One day the Blackbury Dam broke.

The dam was at the end of one of the little valleys

on Even Moor, and it supplied most of Gritshire with water. The news reached Radio Blackbury just as Bertha Fish was about to read the weather forecast, so she and the weathercock piled into the radio car with the reporters and rushed off to see what was going on.

There was a huge crack down one side of the dam and a great stream of water was crashing through the woods further down the valley.

'If the rest of the dam gives way, then Blackbury

will just about be washed out to sea,' said the engineers.

Bits of concrete were already falling into the water and they could hear the fire sirens down in the town as people were warned to run for their lives. Bertha looked at the weathercock, and the weathercock blinked at her. Bertha took a bag of ball bearings from her pocket. The weathercock's

beady eyes lit up. It stretched its neck out and crowed.

And at that very moment, as the whole dam broke, there was a rush of cold wind and a terrific tinkling noise as the water froze solid.

'Brrrr,' said Bertha. 'Well done. There now, we'll just have to saw all that ice into lumps and get rid of it.'

And she and the weathercock went off to read the weather forecast (showery with bright intervals), leaving everyone amazed.

But, of course, that sort of thing happens all the time in Blackbury.

JUDGEMENT DAY FOR FATHER CHRISTMAS

The judge looked down at the prisoner in the dock.

'Why, Father?' he said. 'Are you a religious man of some sort?'

'Not . . . exactly,' said the defendant.

The judge leaned down and whispered to the court usher. 'There appear to be a lot of small people

in pointy hats in the public gallery. Why is this?'

'Friends of the defendant, m'lud. Had to let 'em in, under the new regulations.'

'And the ones with the antlers?'

'Not sure about those, m'lud.'

The judge looked down at his notes. There were 3,433 charges of various offences. He beamed at the jury.

'Well now, ladies and gentlemen,' he said. 'This

has been an interesting case, has it not? I do believe this is the first time in a lengthy career that I have ever heard a defendant plead not guilty on the basis that he isn't really real, or as we would call it in legal terms, On Grounds of Diminished Existence.

'I draw your attention to the succinct evidence of Matthew Higlet, aged seven: "Everyone knows it's just your mum or dad buying presents."

'I also noted Matthew's contention that

although he was good, as agreed, he did not in fact get a' – the judge adjusted his glasses – 'a Sixseveno Mega "Automic Sloth" games console, whatever that is, as promised by the defendant during contract negotiations in, er, Santa's Grotto in the Supermegasaverstore, 34–67 High Street, on 2 December.

'However, in the 1990s we believe in a lot of things which aren't real. Father . . . er . . . Christmas is at least as real as a great many other things I read about in the papers every day, and therefore subject to legislation, just like everyone else.

'Now let us turn to the charges of flying without a licence, endangering air traffic, piloting a vehicle – said vehicle having no certificate of airworthiness – and so on and so forth.

'The police evidence, consisting as it did of

fifteen statements saying "We saw 'im, all right", is very persuasive. But I must draw your attention to this extremely moving film of an experiment conducted by Uppsala University using a herd of reindeer, which started off at the top of a very tall building and ended tragically at the bottom.

'I think it demonstrated very conclusively that the number of reindeer able to fly must be so small as to be statistically insignificant.

'The housebreaking charges, which are numerous, brought forward two interesting defences. We can dismiss Mr . . . Christmas's claim that since he left goods behind, this could not be an offence.

'I'm afraid he does not understand English law. Absolutely anything can be an offence, and frequently is. If people were allowed to go around doing what they like, just because there doesn't happen to be a law against it, we'd be no better than the French.

'But Exhibit C, which contrasts the forty-four-inch waist measurement of the accused with the narrow diameter of the average central-heating flue, offers a very persuasive defence.'

The judge beckoned the usher over again. 'There appear to be more of them. There's even some in the jury box,' he said.

'M'lud?'

'The pointy hats.'

'Are you feeling all right, m'lud?'

'Perhaps I'm just imagining it.'

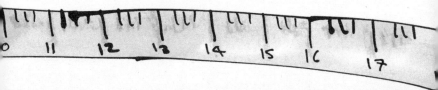

The jury stayed out for quite a long time. The judge spent the time going through the papers for the next day. Things had certainly got busier since the EU directive that quasi-supernatural people were just as answerable to the law as anyone else. That was what equal opportunities was all about.

'It says here,' he said, 'that this woman climbs into people's bedrooms and takes away their teeth, leaving in exchange a small coin of the realm. I suppose we still have a realm, do we? There's been far too much of this sort of thing, and people needn't think they can get away with breaking and entering just because they're called the Tooth Fairy. Why are the jury taking so long?'

'They seem to be having a party, m'lud.'

'And there's a young man here who not only stole a hen and a considerable amount of gold from a giant, but then cut down a beanstalk which almost certainly would be subject to a preservation order. I can see we're going to have a busy year.'

The jury returned, swaying slightly and blowing squeakers.

'How guilty do you find the defendant?' said the judge.

'We don't,' said the foreman of the jury. 'Yippee!'

'I thought as much,' said the judge. 'What is your name?'

'Sneezy, m'lud.'

'I shall probably get into trouble for asking,' said the judge, 'but why did you find the defendant not guilty?'

'It's Christmas, m'lud.'

'Very well, I suppose that was to be expected. Can we please have the reindeer out of the courtroom? Thank you. What's the next case?'

'Attempted murder by means of an armadillo, m'lud.'

'Oh. How dull.'

THE ABOMINABLE
SNOW-BABY

Do you remember the town of Blackbury, and the enormous pie they made especially for Christmas? Well, here's the story of when a particularly snowy day brought to the town a particularly snowy surprise . . .

Visitors to Blackbury often wondered how the great Victorian town hall there was kept so nice and clean. Well, it was because of Albert Scruggins. Albert Scruggins was the caretaker, who lived in the basement with Frambly, the cat, and made endless cups of tea in between stoking the boilers and looking after everything. His father and grandfather had been caretakers before him, and he was pretty proud of living in the town hall, I don't mind telling you.

One day, not long after Christmas, Albert awoke and immediately knew something was wrong. There was a cold smell in the air, and the light that came through the tiny basement window was dim and white.

Snow, he thought. And he didn't think much more about it until he opened the door for the milk.

There was no milk – but a huge wall of snow had started to slide into the town hall. Albert slammed the door and locked it. Then he dashed up to the first floor. The windows were all covered in snow.

Up he climbed to the third floor. Snow.

Up he scrambled, up the narrow ladder to the clock tower on the roof of the town hall, and poked his head out.

It was just like pictures he had seen of the South Pole. Blackbury stretched out all white before him. The gasworks were two white lumps.

The public library was completely hidden under a giant drift. The streets could hardly be told apart from the buildings because they were so full of snow.

It was as quiet and white as the inside of a ping-pong ball.*

Down the stairs ran Albert, with Frambly at his heels. He took his largest spade from the boiler room, opened the door and started to dig. You see, Albert had remembered his granny, who lived on the other side of Blackbury, and

* Though Albert Scruggins had never actually been inside a ping-pong ball, so he did not know if in fact it may have been full of very tiny creatures having a noisy party!

he wanted to make sure that she was all right.

He was making a little white tunnel under the great drifts, and was well away from the town hall when the snow in front of him fell away. He had broken into another tunnel and there, holding a gardening trowel in one hand and a coal shovel in the other, was his granny! She had tennis rackets tied to each of her boots, wore a large woolly hat on her head, and was singing 'Jingle Bells' at the top of her voice.

'Hullo, Albert,' she said. 'I was just coming to see how you were. Brimstone and treacle, but I haven't seen weather like this since I was a girl! I think I shall learn to ski.'

'But you're ninety-eight!' said Albert.

'Prime of life, prime of life, never felt fitter! The mayor's tobogganing on his roof, and everyone's out digging. It's lovely and warm under the snow. Holds the heat in, keeps the cold winds out. We – the serious explorers and adventurers, I mean – have got a fire going in the High Street. We're going to hold a meeting about the snow. Just follow me!'

The snow continued to blow in great drifts around the High Street as Albert Scruggins and his granny reached the huge bonfire. Those who had been able to dig themselves out sat around it, warming their hands and toasting bacon. Somewhere wolves were howling. Everyone looked a bit miserable.

'Great bags of peppermint!'

bellowed Granny, as she burst out of the snow.
'Why don't you have a skiing competition! Don't
sit around like that – it's unhealthy. I think I myself
shall learn to play the trombone.'

Everyone looked even more miserable.

'All the roads are blocked and the telephone lines are down,' said someone, 'and I don't expect anyone will come and dig us out because hardly anyone outside Gritshire knows where Blackbury is.'

'When I was in Alaska during the Gold Rush we had to eat our boots in the end,' said Granny cheerfully. 'Chins up! A good adventure like this might put some backbone into you.'

'Oh dear,' said Albert, thinking of his boots. 'Well, I suppose the first thing we need is an Emergency Squad to dig everyone out of their houses. And then we'd better form an Expedition.'

Just then someone burst out of a snowdrift waving his arms. 'There's a monster down at the gasworks!' he shouted. Then he fell flat on his face in the snow.

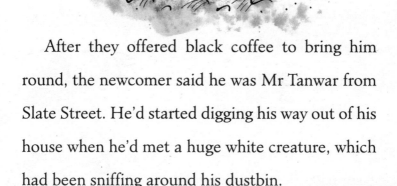

After they offered black coffee to bring him round, the newcomer said he was Mr Tanwar from Slate Street. He'd started digging his way out of his house when he'd met a huge white creature, which had been sniffing around his dustbin.

'It was at least six metres high!' he said.

'Great stuff!' said Granny. 'We've got an **Abominable Snowman!'**

Of course, no one wanted to go and look, but at last Granny persuaded Albert, Mr Tanwar and one or two of the others to set out for Slate Street. They crept along in single file, pushing through the snow, with Granny in the lead clutching her umbrella. When they got to the street, all they found were giant footprints. Each one was nearly a metre across, with three toes.

'Where could the Snowman have come from?' asked Mr Tanwar.

Albert pointed out the white shape of Even Moor, the sinister nearby moorland, just north of Blackbury.

'The footprints go towards it,' he said, 'and there are a lot of places on Even Moor that have never been explored. They say there are still wolves and bears there too.'

'But there are towns and housing estates all around it,' said Mr Tanwar.

'That doesn't make any difference.'

'If you think I'm going up on Even Moor you've got another think to thunk!' said a different voice.

Then what they all thought was a snowdrift got up on its hind legs. They all stood petrified, staring at what was now, very clearly, an Abominable Snowman.

It was staring down at them.

Then it burst into tears.

Albert and the others looked rather embarrassed, but Granny took hold of one huge paw and said, 'There, there . . .' and other soothing things.

'It doesn't look very fierce, I must say,' said Albert.

'It leaped right out at me,' said Mr Tanwar, 'baring its teeth!'

'It hasn't got any teeth,' said Granny. 'Look – just pink gums. I think it's a baby.'

'It's six metres high!' shouted Mr Tanwar.

The Snowman started to cry again, so Granny led it down the street, and it cleared a path through the thick snow. She hooked her umbrella handle round one of its long claws, but everyone who saw them coming leaped over fences and bolted their doors.

When Albert reached his granny's house he found the Snowman asleep on the back lawn, snoring louder than a sawmill. Granny had filled an old tin bathtub full of milk for it, and was now sitting by the fire knitting a giant collar and lead.

'Look, Granny, you can't keep an Abominable Snowman for a pet!'

'He's not at all abominable,' she said sharply. 'He's bominable, and I'm taking him to the Post Office tomorrow to get a pet licence.'

So, of course, Albert had to go with her. And this is what occurred: Granny led the Snowman in through the main entrance. For a moment nothing happened. Then there was a roar and a rip (a sound very similar to the noise made by an Abominable Snowman biting the bottom out of a postmaster's trousers) and suddenly people were jumping out of windows all over the place.

The postmaster himself flew out wearing nothing but his pants,* with the Snowman snapping and galloping after him, and Granny following behind (well, dragged along behind on the lead).

* Very colourful pants they were too, with pink spots and a picture of a cartoon mouse saying something rather rude.

'He called my Snowman a monster!' she cried.

Finally the postmaster climbed a tree, which the Snowman promptly uprooted and shook, and the unfortunate man fell out into a pond.

No postmen would dare go near Granny's house after that. And, as time went by, things got even worse. Granny taught the Abominable Snowman how to do tricks. He would lie on his back and wave his legs in the air like a puppy while she scratched his tummy with a rake. Every morning she used to send him along to the newspaper shop for her paper, and he would bring back the newsagent under one arm.

Then one morning the streets of Blackbury shook to the sound of giant footsteps. Down Blackbury High Street stomped a **giant** Abominable Snow-woman, **growling** and mumbling. She was at least fifty metres high – taller than the church steeple! – and covered in white fur. People were running for their lives and leaping over walls. Except Granny. She didn't even know about the Snow-woman until she took her pet baby Abominable Snowman out for a walk and found the giantess outside her house.

'My word,' she said, 'you're a big one and no mistake!'

With a growl the Snow-woman grabbed her Snow-baby under one arm and Granny under the other and tramped back to Even Moor.

Albert, who had just come to visit his granny, looked on in horror. Then he rushed through the snow to the police station.

'A whacking great snow creature has just stolen my granny!' he gasped.

'Now then, now then,' said the sergeant, 'would you care to give me a description of the missing article?'

'About five foot tall, red face, white hair, a black hat with pins in it, and button boots,' said Albert. 'She's been taken to Even Moor by a monster!'

Soon a group of police officers and a few of the braver townspeople were following the trail of the Snow-woman through the snowbound streets. The giant footprints led up to Even Moor, where the snow was piled in eerie drifts and the wind whistled.

Now Even Moor, although in the centre of the county of Gritshire and surrounded by towns and neat farms, was well known to be one of those few places that had survived unchanged from the dawn of history. There were said to be witches and werewolves there, and giants and brontosauri, all living in its low hills and little woods. It was getting dark and, one by one, the police officers and townspeople following the trail started remembering appointments and hurrying home. In fact, Albert was the only one of the group left when the footprints led to the entrance of a little cave.

He tiptoed very slowly up to it and peered in.

The Snow-woman was sitting with her baby in her arms and grunting a snowy lullaby, while Granny was shaking a rattle for it.

'Hullo, grandson,' she said. 'Be quiet or you'll wake the baby.'

'I thought you were being torn to pieces!' gasped Albert.

'Nonsense!' said Granny. 'We get on like a house on fire. I've just given her a few hints on baby care. While there's still snow all over Europe, she's off tomorrow to travel to India, to join her husband on Mount Everest.'

Then Albert and his granny quietly slipped away from the cave and back to snowy Blackbury.

'He was a nice little pet,' said Granny thoughtfully.

Albert smiled.

THE TWELVE GIFTS OF CHRISTMAS

Once upon a time – that's always a good start –
there was a young prince who was ruler of the
Land of the Sun. It was a pleasant country of
long days and blue skies, and most things in it
were either yellow or gold.

The cottages were built of sandstone with golden tiles; daffodils and buttercups grew in fields of ripe corn, and gold was so plentiful under the land that the streets were actually paved with it.

Now, to the west of this land was a high range of mountains, where the prince – did I say his name was Alfred? Well, it was – had a hunting lodge.

One day when he was out hunting deer with his knights his horse bolted, and carried him away

through the thick pine forests. The sounds of the hunt disappeared in the distance, while the prince leaned on the reins and tried to calm his mount.

By the time he had done this he was in an unknown part of the mountains, on the edge of a wide clearing. He found what was wrong with his horse – a sharp thorn had got under the saddle girth – and while he stood adjusting it a deer burst into the centre of the glade.

It was the one he had been hunting – but before he could reach for his bow a silver arrow hissed out of the trees and killed the creature.

Oi, oi, he thought. Poachers in my mountains!

Out of the trees rode a host of knights in silver armour, riding white horses. At their head rode a princess clad in silver cloth.

She had white hair, and I daresay I hardly have to tell you that Alfred thought she was the dearest, prettiest, fairest, etc., princess he'd ever clapped eyes on, even though her long hair was whiter than his granny's.

Her knights took the deer and rode away, and of course Alfred followed. He soon realized that he was going down the other side of the mountain.

The sun was setting, and this is what he saw.

Over the land on the other side of the mountains a big silver moon was rising. The whole land shone like silver, silver flowers grew in the grass, and in the distance his princess was riding.

'Where is this place?' the prince wondered
out loud.

In the tree above, someone coughed.

'It's the Land of the Moon, of course.'

The prince looked up and saw that he was under an old wild pear tree, with gnarled boughs and wizened fruit, and hardly any leaves to speak of. On the lowest branch sat a large, fat, ugly brown bird with big eyebrows.

'What sort of bird is it that speaks?' said Alfred.

'Me. I'm the partridge. *The* Partridge, I should say, In A Pear Tree. And you're Prince Alfred.

'The girl is Princess Selena, but if you want to marry her you'll have to woo her. Chocolates and flowers and so on.'

'She looks as though she can have anything she wants,' pointed out Alfred.

'Please yourself,' said the partridge. 'I'm only here to help, I'm sure. All I'll say is she has promised to marry the first man that gives her a Christmas present that dances, leaps, plays tunes, makes a beat, carries pails, hisses, swims, lays eggs, can be worn on one hand, sings, cackles, coos, waggles its eyebrows and is good to eat. All at once, let me add.'

'What for?' asked Prince Alfred.

'Her father, King of the Land of the Moon, decided that only the man who could think up the right kind of present was worthy to marry his daughter. He's got no son, you see, so whoever is her husband will become king of that land in time,' added the partridge.

'A parrot,' said the prince thoughtfully. 'That might be all right.'

'The Emperor of the Rainbow Land tried that,' said the partridge. 'It didn't work.'

So the prince said goodbye to the wise old

partridge in his pear tree, and went back home deep in thought.

He called all the palace wizards, wise men and deep thinkers together, and he asked them, 'What dances, leaps, plays tunes, makes a beat, carries pails, hisses, swims, lays eggs, can be worn on one hand, sings, cackles, coos, waggles its eyebrows and is good to eat? Come on, work it out, or you'll get no Christmas bonus!' He paused. 'The person who can answer this will also win a big golden cup!'

'It's a riddle,' said one of the wizards. But think as they might, they couldn't find the answer. And

so the competition was open to everyone in the
Land of the Sun.

Now, although the hall of the castle was soon
filled to overflowing with postmen sorting out
the replies, and people queuing up in the hope of
winning the cup, no one thought up anything like
the right answer. The prince sat on his gold throne
and sighed.

Right at the end of the queue one day was the
partridge, walking since he was far too fat to fly.
'What are you doing here!'
gasped Prince Alfred.

'I've come for the prize,' said the partridge.

'You mean you knew all the time?'

'You didn't ask me, did you? But I don't want the
cup. What I want costs nothing, is as light as air,
and I shan't tell you what it is. Not yet, anyway.'

'What is the present I'm to give the princess, then?' asked Prince Alfred.

'Patience, patience,' said the partridge. 'I want to have a meeting with some of your subjects first. Kindly call for the Royal Swankeeper, the Guardian of the Crown Jewels, the Master of the Royal Music, the highest Lord in the land, the chief Lady-in-Waiting, and about four farmers. I'll need them all to make the present.

'Then I want you to go and visit the princess, and her father, and bring them to my pear tree in the mountains.'

This the prince did, though he wondered what the partridge had in store.

He went to the Land of the Moon, and brought the king and the princess and a host of their knights up to the pear tree.

'What sort of present is this?' said the king. 'The pears are good to eat, maybe, but nothing else. They don't sing.'

'Wait just a moment,' said the prince, gazing anxiously down the road.

'I'm not waiting here all day,' said the king angrily. 'Show me the present you've got for my daughter or be off.'

'Wait a minute, Father,' said Princess Selena.

'There's something coming!'

Prince Alfred looked down the road at the approaching cloud of dust and then let out a whoop of joy.

A very odd crowd could now be seen.

In the lead was a small boy called Bert, the son of the Royal Swankeeper, carrying three

enormous cages. One contained two sulky turtle doves, the next three French hens, and the biggest, which kept bumping against his knees, held four little green birds.

On Bert's head sat the partridge, holding on tightly to his hair and shouting instructions to the others. His voice was rather muffled since he was also trying to hold five large gold rings in his beak.

After Bert came the Royal Swankeeper himself, herding seven hissing swans and six waddling geese, who kept getting under the feet of the eight milkmaids who were puffing along behind.

After them came a big drum, bowling along with its drummer galloping after it, and the other eight drummers hotly in pursuit, closely followed by ten pipers who played as they ran.

Eleven lords came leaping after them, robes flying, and bringing up the rear was a carriage holding twelve ladies-in-waiting.

'Now you all know what you've got to do,' said the partridge, when they reached the old pear tree. And pears rained down as everyone scrambled up into the branches, treading on fingers and cracking branches.

'Quick, quick!' said the partridge. 'Are we all

ready? Now tell the princess what her present is.'

'**Twelve ladies dancing,**' said

the ladies on the lowest branch.

'**Eleven lords a-leaping,**'

sang the lords, rocketing up and down through

the tree. **Creak!**

Rattle!

'**Ten pipers piping** – one, two,

one two three four,' sang the pipers, and went

into a spirited rendering of the tune.

'**Nine drummers drumming!**'

Thud!

Boom!

'Eight maids a-milking.'

'Hiss! Hiss!' went the seven swans, who couldn't a-swim on their branch and were angry about it.

'Honk! Honk!' went the six geese a-laying.

'Ring! Ting!' sang the five gold rings in the wind.

'Call! Chirrup!' sang the four calling birds.

'Le Cackle!' cackled the three French hens.

'Coo! Coo!' sang the two turtle doves.

There was a breathless pause, and everyone

stared up at the partridge. He made sure they were all watching, then ruffled his feathers, stretched out his wings, and with a voice like sandpaper sang: 'And a partridge in a pearrrrrrr' – his neck stretched and his face went red as he took a deep breath –

treeeeeeeee!

The silence that followed was broken by the laughter of the king, who sat on his horse with tears running down his face.

'It's the funniest thing I've seen in years,' he said. 'And it does everything it should do! Marry my daughter by all means!'

'I think it's a lovely present,' said the princess.

'Cough, cough,' said the partridge tactfully, from his position on the topmost branch. 'My reward is that I want to sing a song that I've invented about all this at your wedding.'

'Yes,' said the prince. 'You must all come!'

So – on the Twelfth Day of Christmas, as it happened – they held a great wedding party in a large tent erected over the old pear tree in the mountains, and the partridge sang his song and was made Prime Minister on the spot by the prince.

Several of the smaller pipers ate too much, and had to be sent home in wheelbarrows, but the prince gave everyone medals and they were all very happy.

FATHER CHRISTMAS GOES TO WORK AT THE ZOO

Father Christmas lay fast asleep on the sofa with a newspaper over his face, and occasionally he snored a little. Mrs Christmas was sitting on the other side of the roaring fire, darning his socks and talking.

'...**And I'm getting fed up!**

You only work one evening a year these days,

and even if you do get paid overtime there's the reindeer to feed. It's about time you got a new job, my lad.'

'Eh? What?' said Father Christmas, sitting up.

'A new job,' said Mrs Christmas, starting another sock. 'Something that'll bring in a little extra cash and keep you out from under my feet all day. You might even enjoy it.'

'Well, I don't know about that,' said Father Christmas, stroking his beard. 'A man in my position, you know, has certain responsibilities . . .'

Then he thought: She's got a point. I always wanted to be an engine driver when I was a little lad. I wonder what else I *could* do?

So next morning he dusted off his old grey suit (he usually wore a red one with white fur here and there) and Mrs Christmas made sandwiches for him, and then off he went to look for a job.

'Are you really Father Christmas?' said the man at the Job Centre in amazement. 'Well, well! I remember you brought me a train set when I was nine.'*

'Ah, yes, I recall it well,' said Father Christmas, sitting down. The job man started to fill in a form.

'You say you can fly, but you haven't got a pilot's licence. You go into people's houses by climbing down chimneys, but frankly that sounds a bit burglarous. You give things away. Hmm. Oh dear, I don't know. Very difficult. I suppose you don't have

*Actually, that year, Father Christmas brought *every* nine-year-old a train set.

much experience in looking after animals?'

Father Christmas, who had been looking very glum, brightened up. 'Certainly,' he said. 'Reindeer and polar bears and so forth.'

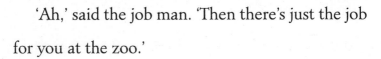

'Ah,' said the job man. 'Then there's just the job for you at the zoo.'

'What's a zoo?'

'They keep animals there, to help to understand them and save those in danger of dying out. I imagine it's great fun: just go and say I sent you and they'll probably even give you a uniform!'

Next day Father Christmas went to start work at Blackbury Zoo.

About two hours later the man at the job agency got a phone call

which went on for a very long time (just as if the person on the other end was **very, very angry**).

Just as he put the telephone down Father Christmas shuffled in sheepishly, still wearing his zoo uniform.

'Well,' said the job man severely, 'it's a fine mess you've made of *that*.'

'I know,' said Father Christmas in a small voice.

'You let the **monkeys** out—'

'I know.'

'You gave everyone **free elephant rides**.'

'I felt so sorry for them, you see. And the elephants enjoyed it . . .'

'And you taught the **hippos to fly**. Very dangerous things, flying hippos.'*

'They didn't have any reindeer, you see,' said Father Christmas miserably.

* Last seen heading over the English Channel in the direction of Africa. The hippos had got fed up with being studied and saved, and fancied saving themselves.

'I don't know, I'm sure. Can't you think of any other job you could do?' said the job man.

'I'd like to be an astronaut or a cowboy,' said Father Christmas.

'Um,' said the job man. 'Not much call for

those. How about selling ice cream? There's a job here for an ice-cream man . . .'

Two hours later Father Christmas gingerly drove out of the Blackbury ice-cream factory in a bright yellow and pink van with **Mr Brrr** written on the side. He stopped at a likely-looking spot and soon lots of children were queuing up for ice cream.

'A small ice-cream cornet, please,' said the first one.

Father Christmas filled it and looked at it in dismay. 'That's not very much ice cream,' he said, so he scooped two more big dollops onto the cone, and added a wafer, two chocolate thingummyjigs and half a dozen cherries. 'There,' he said, beaming. 'You can have this for twenty pence.'

The little boy looked at it in amazement – and soon there was a big crowd around the van. Father Christmas was having the time of his life, building huge great creamy cones covered with all sorts of twirls, swirls, cherries* and wafers. And selling them for next to nothing or even less.

* At last! A use for all those glacé cherries.

This is just the job for me, he thought happily.

'Well,' said the job man, 'this is another fine mess you've got me into.'

'I'm sorry,' said Father Christmas mournfully.

'According to the manager of the ice-cream company, you got rid of one hundred pounds' worth of ice cream for seven pounds. They're very, very **angry**,' said the job man sternly, looking at his notes. 'Isn't there anything you can do without making a mess of it?'

Father Christmas, who was really very sorry and quite sad, blew his nose loudly. 'It seemed such a shame to take the kiddies' money,' he explained.

'Look, the only other job we've got that would suit you is one as a gardener,' said the job man more kindly. 'A healthy, outdoor life in Blackbury Parks and Gardens Department. That'd suit you, I expect, and I don't think there's any trouble you could possibly get into.'

So next day Father Christmas started work in one of the municipal greenhouses, and for a while it looked as though he was doing very well. Being a sort of old-fashioned wizard, you see, he was very good at getting things to grow, and he quite enjoyed pottering about pruning and planting.

'You're doing very well, Mr Christmas,' said the head gardener a few days later. 'In fact, I think you can plant out the **big** flower bed down by the town hall tomorrow. The ornamental one, you know.'

Father Christmas knew it. Every month or so they used to change the flowers so the colours spelled out names, or made the borough coat of arms, or something interesting like that.

'We'll leave the choice of design up to you,' said the head gardener. 'Something tasteful in primroses, perhaps?'

Father Christmas had a bit of a think, and later he set off with his gardening tools and a big wheelbarrow. He put a canvas screen round the flower bed and set to work. It was getting on for tea time when he stopped.

A few minutes later the head gardener came along to see how he had got on. When she saw the flower bed she stopped and her mouth dropped open in amazement.

'Don't you like it?' said Father Christmas nervously.

'You've spelled out "Merry Christmas" in flowers!' blurted out the head gardener. 'But Christmas is eleven months away! We can't have this sort of thing, you know.'

'I thought it might cheer people up,' said Father Christmas. 'I suppose I'm sacked?'

'I'm afraid the mayor will insist on it after he sees that,' said the gardener.

So Father Christmas trooped off to see the job man, who looked up from his files and said,

'What, you again?'

'There was a bit of a disagreement over a flower bed, you see.'

'I don't really see, but anyway, all the jobs that are going now are for steamroller drivers and bakers, and I dread to think of you doing either of them.'

He gave Father Christmas a form to fill in in case any jobs cropped up, and then the old man went home. Mrs Christmas was washing his red suit ready for December.

'I don't seem to be any good at anything,' said Father Christmas, taking his boots off.

'I just don't know how we're going to manage until next Christmas,' said Mrs Christmas.

Just then there was a knock at the door. It was the job man, very breathless, holding the form that

Father Christmas had filled in.

'Why didn't you tell me you were six hundred years old?' he said.

'Is it important then?'

'Of course – you ought to be getting the State Pension! Come to think of it, you ought to get a bit for the five hundred and thirty-five years you missed too. That'd be thousands and thousands of pounds!'

'A State Pension?' wondered Father Christmas. 'Fancy that! Come in and have a cup of tea!'

And so they did.

Read more from the

The fantastically funny

TERRY PRATCHETT

Imagine that all around you, hidden from sight, there are **thousands** of **tiny people**. They are **four inches tall**, **brave**, **stubborn** and **resourceful**.

They are the **nomes** – and this is the first book of their **adventures**:

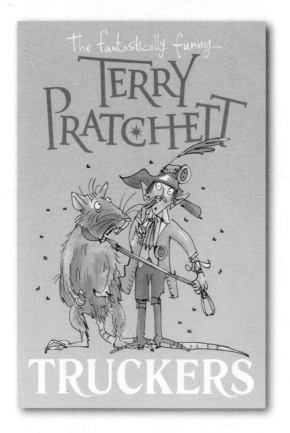

The fantastically funny

TERRY PRATCHETT

TRUCKERS

Turn the page for an **opening extract** . . .

CONCERNING NOMES AND TIME

Nomes are small. On the whole, small creatures don't live for a long time. But perhaps they do live *fast*. Let me explain.

One of the shortest-lived creatures on the planet Earth is the adult common mayfly. It lasts for one day. The longest-living things are bristlecone pine trees, at 4,700 years and still counting.

This may seem tough on mayflies. But the important thing is not how long your life is, but how long it seems.

To a mayfly, a single hour may last as long as a century. Perhaps old mayflies sit around complaining about how life this minute isn't a patch on the good old minutes of long ago, when the world was young and the sun seemed so much brighter and larvae showed you a bit of respect. Whereas the trees, which are not famous for their quick reactions, may just have time to notice the way the sky keeps flickering before the dry rot and woodworm set in.

It's all a sort of relativity. The faster you live, the more time stretches out. To a nome, a year lasts as long as ten years does to a human. Remember it. Don't let it concern you. They don't. They don't even know.

In the beginning . . .

I.   There was the Site.
II.   And Arnold Bros (est. 1905) Moved upon the face
      of the Site, and Saw that it had Potential.
III. For it was In the High Street.
IV.   Yea, it was also Handy for the Buses.
V.   And Arnold Bros (est. 1905) said, Let there be a Store,
      And Let it be a Store such as the World has not Seen
      hitherto;
VI.   Let the length of it be from Palmer Street even unto the
      Fish Market, and the Width of It, from the High Street
      right back to Disraeli Road;
VII. Let it be High even Unto Five Storeys plus Basement,
      And bright with Lifts; let there be the Eternal Fires of the
      Boiler-Room in the sub-basement and, above all other floors,
      let there be Customer Accounts to Order All Things;
VIII. For this must be what all shall Know of Arnold Bros
      (est.1905): All Things Under One Roof. And it shall be called:
      the Store of Arnold Bros (est. 1905).
IX.   And Thus it Was.
X.   And Arnold Bros (est. 1905) divided the Store into
      Departments, of Ironmongery, Corsetry, Modes and others
      After their Kind, and Created Humans to fill them with All
      Things saying, Yea, All Things Are Here. And Arnold Bros
      (est. 1905) said, Let there be Lorries, and Let their Colours
      be Red and Gold, and Let them Go Forth so that All May
      Know Arnold Bros (est. 1905), By Appointment, delivers
      All Things;
XI.   Let there be Santa's Grottoes and Winter Sales and Summer
      Bargains and Back to School Week and All Commodities in
      their Season;
XII. And into the Store came the Nomes, that it would be their
      Place, for Ever and Ever.

From The Book of Nome, Basements v.I–XII

CHAPTER ONE

This is the story of the Going Home.

This is the story of the Critical Path.

This is the story of the lorry roaring through the sleeping city and out into the country lanes, smashing through street lamps and swinging from side to side and shattering shop windows and rolling to a halt when the police chased it. And when the baffled men went back to their car to report *Listen, will you, listen? There isn't anyone driving it!*, it became the story of the lorry that started up again, rolled away from the astonished men, and vanished into the night.

But the story didn't end there.

It didn't start there, either.

*   *   *

The sky rained dismal. It rained humdrum. It rained the kind of rain that is so much wetter than normal rain, the kind of rain that comes down in big drops and splats, the kind of rain that is merely an upright sea with slots in it.

It rained a tattoo on the old hamburger boxes and chip papers in the wire basket that was giving Masklin a temporary hiding place.

Look at him. Wet. Cold. Extremely worried. And four inches high.

The waste-bin was usually a good hunting ground, even in winter. There were often a few cold chips in their wrapping, sometimes even a chicken bone. Once or twice there had been a rat too. It had been a really good day when there had last been a rat – it had kept them going for a week. The trouble was that you could get pretty fed up with rat by the third day. By the third mouthful, come to that.

Masklin scanned the lorry park.

And here it came, right on time, crashing through the puddles and pulling up with a hiss of brakes.

He'd watched this lorry arrive every Tuesday and

Thursday morning for the last four weeks. He timed the driver's stop carefully.

They had exactly three minutes. To someone the size of a nome, that's more than half an hour.

He scrambled down through the greasy paper, dropped out of the bottom of the bin, and ran for the bushes at the edge of the park where Grimma and the old folk were waiting.

'It's here!' he said. 'Come on!'

They got to their feet, groaning and grumbling. He'd taken them through this dozens of times. He knew it wasn't any good shouting. They just got upset and confused, and then they'd grumble some more. They grumbled about cold chips, even when Grimma warmed them up. They moaned about rat. He'd seriously thought about leaving alone, but he couldn't bring himself to do it. They needed him. They needed someone to grumble at.

But they were too *slow*. He felt like bursting into tears.

He turned to Grimma instead.

'Come *on*,' he said. 'Give them a prod, or something. They'll never get moving!'

She patted his hand.

'They're frightened,' she said. 'You go on. I'll bring them out.'

There wasn't time to argue. Masklin ran back across the soaking mud of the park, unslinging the rope and grapnel. It had taken him a week to make the hook, out of a bit of wire teased off a fence, and he'd spent days practising; he was already swinging it around his head as he reached the lorry's wheel.

The hook caught the tarpaulin high above him at the second try. He tested it once or twice and then, his feet scrabbling for a grip on the tyre, pulled himself up.

He'd done it before. Oh, he'd done it three or four times. He scrambled under the heavy tarpaulin and into the darkness beyond, pulling out more line and tying it as tightly as possible around one of the ropes that were as thick as his arm.

Then he slid back to the edge and, thank goodness, Grimma *was* herding the old people across the gravel. He could hear them complaining about the puddles.

Masklin jumped up and down with impatience.

It seemed to take hours. He explained it to them millions of times, but people hadn't been pulled up onto the backs of lorries when they were children and they didn't see why they should start now. Old Granny Morkie insisted that all the men look the other way so that they wouldn't see up her skirts, for example, and old Torrit whimpered so much that Masklin had to lower him again so that Grimma could blindfold him. It wasn't so bad after he'd hauled the first few up, because they were able to help on the rope, but time still stretched out.

He pulled Grimma up last. She was light. They were *all* light, if it came to that. You didn't get rat every day.

It was amazing. They were all on board. He'd worked with an ear cocked for the sound of footsteps on gravel and the slamming of the driver's door, and it hadn't happened.

'Right,' he said, shaking with the effort. 'That's it, then. Now if we just go—'

'I dropped the Thing,' said old Torrit. 'The Thing. I dropped it, d'you see? I dropped it down by the wheel when she was blindfoldin' me. You go and get it, boy.'

Masklin looked at him in horror. Then he poked

his head out from under the tarpaulin and, yes, there it was, far below. A tiny black cube on the ground.

The Thing.

It was lying in a puddle, although that wouldn't affect it. Nothing touched the Thing. It wouldn't even burn.

And then he heard the sound of slow footsteps on the gravel.

'There's no time,' he whispered. 'There really is no time.'

'We can't go without it,' said Grimma.

'Of course we can. It's just a, a thing. We won't need the wretched object where we're going.'

He felt guilty as soon as he'd said it, amazed at his own lips for uttering such words. Grimma looked horrified. Granny Morkie drew herself up to her full, quivering height.

'May you be forgiven!' she barked. 'What a terrible thing to say! You tell him, Torrit.' She nudged Torrit in the ribs.

'If we ain't taking the Thing, I ain't going,' said Torrit sulkily. 'It's not—'

'That's your leader talkin' to you,' interrupted

Granny Morkie. 'So you do what you're told. Leave it behind, indeed! It wouldn't be decent. It wouldn't be right. So you go and get it, this minute.'

Masklin stared wordlessly down at the soaking mud and then, with a desperate motion, threw the line over the edge and slid down it.

It was raining harder now, with a touch of sleet. The wind whipped at him as he dropped past the great arc of the wheel and landed heavily in the puddle. He reached out and scooped up the Thing—

And the lorry started to move.

First there was a roar, so loud that it went beyond sound and became a solid wall of noise. Then there was a blast of stinking air and a vibration that shook the ground.

He pulled sharply on the line and yelled at them to pull him up, and realized that even he couldn't hear his own voice. But Grimma or someone must have got the idea because, just as the big wheel began to turn, the rope tightened and he felt his feet lifted off the mud.

He bounced and spun back and forth as, with painful slowness, they pulled him past the wheel. It turned only a few inches away from him, a black, chilly blur, and all the time the hammering sound battered at his head.

I'm not scared, he told himself. This is much worse than anything I've ever faced, and it's not frightening. It's too terrible to be frightening.

He felt as though he was in a tiny, warm cocoon, away from all the noise and the wind. I'm going to die, he thought, just because of this Thing which has never helped us at all, something that's just a lump of stuff, and now I'm going to die and go to the Heavens. I wonder if old Torrit is right about what happens when you die? It seems a bit severe to have to die to find out. I've looked at the sky every night for years and I've never seen any nomes up there . . .

But it didn't really matter, it was all outside him, it wasn't real—

Hands reached down and caught him under the arms and dragged him into the booming space under the tarpaulin and, with some difficulty, prised the Thing out of his grip.

Behind the speeding lorry fresh curtains of grey rain dragged across the empty fields.

And, across the whole country, there were no more nomes.

**Look out for more short-story
collections from the wonderful**

TERRY PRATCHETT

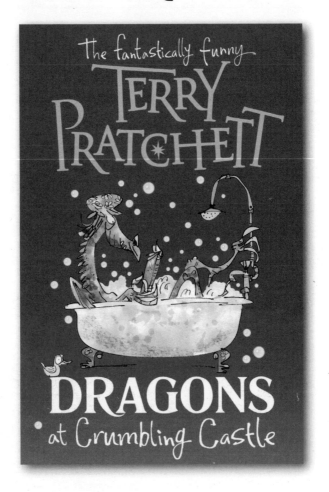

From **castles** and **chaos** . . .

... to **magic** and **mayhem!**